How To Speak
MOO!

Loud

Soft

Jiggly

Boinging

In a tunnel

Through a funnel

Wobbly

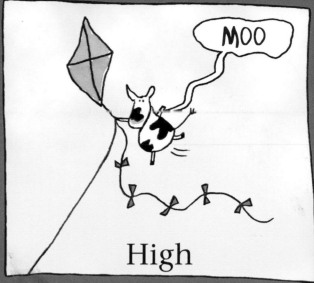

High

Low

Moo–sical

Smooth

Sleeping

To all the cows.
And a big Mooo to Lina, Joe, Renate, Saul, David,
Rachel, Heather, Elaine, Caroline and Eliz.

HOW TO SPEAK MOO!
A RED FOX BOOK 9781862308718

First published in Great Britain by Hutchinson,
an imprint of Random House Children's Books

Hutchinson edition published 2002
Red Fox edition published 2003

5 7 9 10 8 6 4

Red Fox Books are published by Random House Children's Books,
61–63 Uxbridge Road, London W5 5SA,
a division of The Random House Group Ltd,
in Australia by Random House Australia (Pty) Ltd,
20 Alfred Street, Milsons Point, Sydney, NSW 2061, Australia,
in New Zealand by Random House New Zealand Ltd,
18 Poland Road, Glenfield, Auckland 10, New Zealand,
and in South Africa by Random House (Pty) Ltd,
Endulini, 5A Jubilee Road, Parktown 2193, South Africa

THE RANDOM HOUSE GROUP Limited Reg. No. 954009
www.kidsatrandomhouse.co.uk

A CIP catalogue record for this book is available from the British Library.

Printed in Singapore

HOW TO SPEAK

MOO!

Deborah Fajerman

RED FOX

The cow language is called Moo
and every single word is moo.

So, you think that all moos
sound the same?
Well, think again.

Moo can be so loud
it is heard from miles around.

And Moo can be so soft
you hardly hear a sound.

When cows jump on a trampoline
their moos go up and down.

And when they go to sleep
their moos lie on the ground.

Cows don't make any noise at all
when they watch the telly.

But Moo sounds very wobbly
when they wobble on a jelly.

Cows never moo when they eat their lunch. The sound they make is munch munch munch munch.

A cow in a sailing boat gently moves
which makes its moo extremely smooth.

Cow on skateboard – path is lumpy.

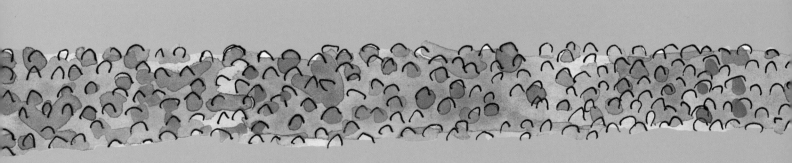

Cow is jiggly – moo is jumpy.

The language cows know best is Moo.
But they know some other words too.

High moo, low moo, soft moo, loud moo,
All-together moos make the very best...

Loud

Soft

Jiggly

Boinging

In a tunnel

Through a funnel

Wobbly

High

Low

Moo–sical

Smooth

Sleeping

OTHER BOOKS YOU MIGHT ENJOY:

Cinderella's Bum

by Nicholas Allan

Egg Drop

by Mini Grey

George and the Dragon

by Chris Wormell

Next Please

by Ernst Jandl and Norman Junge

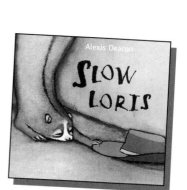

Poochie-Poo

by Helen Stephens

Slow Loris

by Alexis Deacon

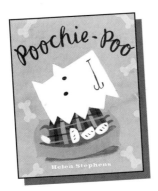

Tiny

by Paul Rogers and Korky Paul